GEORGE

Visits the Doctor

GEO

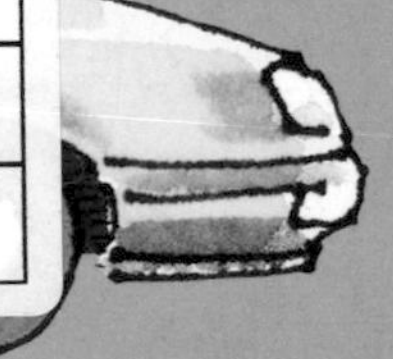

Nicola Smee

RGE

Visits the Doctor

I've got a sore throat
and so has Bear.

Mum's taking us
to see the doctor.

"Open wide and say, Aah!" says Doctor.

Aaah!
Aaah!

He looks into our ears
with a little torch.

"Take a deep breath,"
says Doctor, and
he listens to our
chests with his
stethoscope.

"Bear's fine, but this medicine will soon make you better, George," says Doctor.

Goodbye,
Doctor!

"Here you are, George,"
says the chemist.
"Let me give this to
your mum."

"Time for your medicine," says Mum. "You'll soon be well again."

George's
Medicine

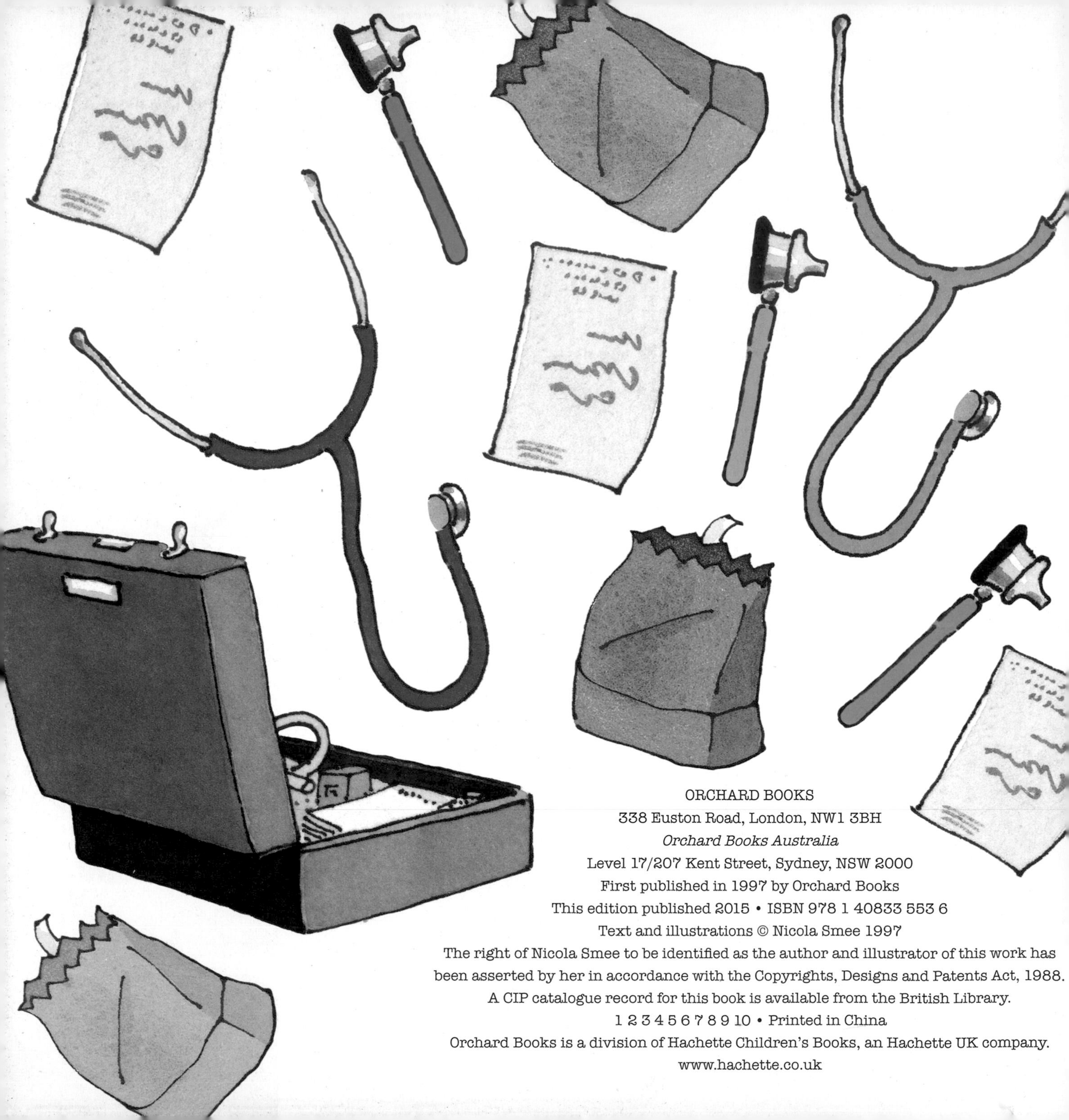

ORCHARD BOOKS
338 Euston Road, London, NW1 3BH
Orchard Books Australia
Level 17/207 Kent Street, Sydney, NSW 2000
First published in 1997 by Orchard Books
This edition published 2015 • ISBN 978 1 40833 553 6

A CIP catalogue record for this book is available from the British Library.
1 2 3 4 5 6 7 8 9 10 • Printed in China
Orchard Books is a division of Hachette Children's Books, an Hachette UK company.
www.hachette.co.uk